E
CRE

Crebbin, June.

Danny's duck.

$13.95

000028506
03/05/1997

DATE			

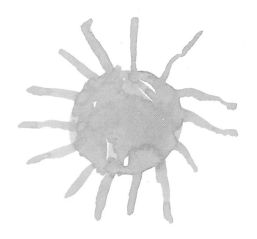

For Sally
J.C.

For Liz
C.V.

Text copyright © 1995 by June Crebbin
Illustrations copyright © 1995 by Clara Vulliamy

First U.S. edition 1995
Published in Great Britain in 1995 by Walker Books Ltd., London.

Library of Congress Cataloging-in-Publication Data

Crebbin, June.
Danny's duck / written by June Crebbin ; illustrated by Clara Vulliamy.—1st U.S. ed.
"Published in Great Britain in 1995 by Walker Books Ltd., London"—T.p. verso.
Summary: Danny regularly visits a mother duck and her nest near his school playground,
and then one day something wonderful happens.
ISBN 1-56402-536-5 (reinforced trade ed.)
[1. Ducks—Fiction. 2. Schools—Fiction.] I. Vulliamy, Clara, ill. II. Title.
PZ7.C86Dan   1995
[E]—dc20   94-10434

10 9 8 7 6 5 4 3 2 1

Printed in Italy

The pictures in this book were done in watercolor.

Candlewick Press
2067 Massachusetts Avenue
Cambridge, Massachusetts 02140

Danny's Duck

June Crebbin

illustrated by

Clara Vulliamy

CANDLEWICK PRESS
CAMBRIDGE, MASSACHUSETTS

A duck flew over the land,
looking for a good woody place.
Down she flew to a pile of brushwood
at the edge of a school playground.

No one saw her come . . .

except Danny.

At playtime he looked for her.
He had to look hard. Her colors
were so much like the colors of the twigs
and branches. But Danny saw her.

And she saw him.

In school Danny drew the duck sitting.

"How lovely," said his teacher. "A duck on her nest."

When Danny visited the pile of
brushwood again, the duck was still there,
sitting very still. Again she saw him.
Then she stood up and stretched.

Danny saw her eggs.
He looked and counted.

In school he drew a picture of the nest
with nine pale green eggs in it.

"How lovely," said his teacher.
"Eggs. With ducklings inside, growing."

Danny visited the duck every day.
Children played in the playground.
Parents passed close by on the footpath.
But no one saw.

One sunny morning, just as he always did,
Danny ran onto the playground and over
to the pile of brushwood.

But the duck wasn't there.
Neither were her eggs.
The nest was empty.

Danny cried.
He cried and cried.

In school he drew a picture of the empty nest.
But when his teacher saw the picture, she smiled!

"The mother duck eats the eggshells after the eggs have hatched," she said.

At lunchtime, Danny took his teacher
across the playground to the pile of brushwood.

There was the nest.

Then his teacher took Danny
across the school field to the pond.

Danny looked.

"There's my duck!" he shouted.
"And—one, two, three, four, five,
six, seven, eight, *nine ducklings!*"

And everyone came to see.